For Poppy and Coco

THE NAUGHTIEST REINDEER

REINDEER

Goes South

Nicki Greenberg

ALLEN&UNWIN
SYDNEY • MELBOURNE • AUCKLAND • LONDON

On the night before Christmas, the reindeer were ready,
The jingle-bells shining, the sleigh runners steady.
The presents were sorted, and Santa felt fine…

But – oh dear! What's that fuss at the front of the line?

Ruby the reindeer and Rudolf, her brother,
Were stamping and snorting and *shoving* each other!
'Not fair!' shouted Ruby. 'It's *my* turn this year!'
'Not a chance,' replied Rudolf. 'Step down, little deer.'

'But Rudolf!' cried Ruby, 'I'm faster! I'm stronger!
So what if you've been in the business for longer?
I'm zippy! I'm snappy! I'm raring to go—'

'You're NAUGHTY,' said Rudolf. 'The answer is NO.'

'Enough!' Mrs Claus said. 'There's no time to fight.
Squeeze up now, you two. You can *both* lead tonight.
And Ruby? I know that you're bright and you're brave.
But listen here, dear: *you had better behave.*'

And did Ruby behave?
That depends what you mean.

She behaved…

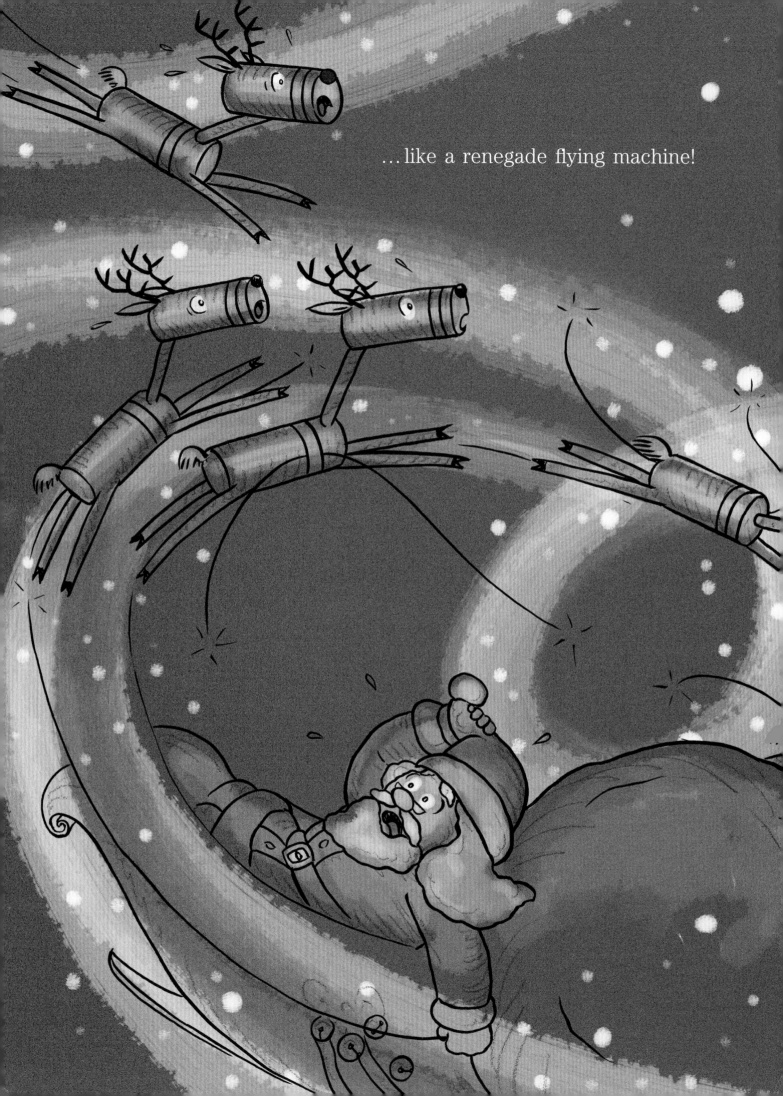

...like a renegade flying machine!

She swooped and she swerved. She cornered and spun.
She shouted out, 'SHORTCUT! WOOHOO! THIS IS FUN!'
She looped and she leapt, and she raced on ahead…

'SLOW DOWN!' bellowed Santa.
'YOU'LL CAPSIZE THE SLED!'

Dive, Dasher! Dive, Dancer! Dive, Prancer and Vixen!
Go, Comet! Go, Cupid! Go, Donner and Blitzen!

'Great work, champs!' cried Rudolf. 'You've rescued the lot.'

But *had* they?

Oh, *frankincense* ...
No. They had *not*.

'Hey, guys! Over here!
Hey, Rudolf! Hello?
Come back! Come and get me! I'm stuck in the snow!'

But nobody answered. The whole team had flown.
And Ruby was left, in the cold, all alone.

Well ... not quite ...

A flurry of flippers. An angry commotion.
Strange creatures were swarming up out of the ocean.
'What *are* you?' they cried, as they circled the deer.
'And *why* have you dumped all this rubbish round here?'

'Rubbish?' gasped Ruby. 'No, no! These are toys!
Presents – for Christmas – for young girls and boys.
They all tumbled down when I tipped Santa's sleigh:
I must get them back to him now, right away!
If you could just point me towards the North Pole,
Mrs Claus will soon have this all under control.'

'WHAT???'

'North?' laughed the penguins. 'You've got the wrong end!
This is Antarctica. South-side, my friend.
And as for your tale of a flying toboggan?
What nonsense! That fall must have scrambled your noggin.
Wherever you're from, take your litter back *there*.'

And they waddled away,
with their beaks in the air.

Ruby stared miserably out at the sea.
'Those kids will miss Christmas, and all thanks to me.'
A little tear froze as it dripped down her face.
'And how will I ever get out of this place?'

Meanwhile, on a beach, far away...

Santa Claus sighed as he sat on the shore.
'I don't think I'm fit for this job anymore.
I've run out of stock, and that deer's done a bunk.
I'm sorry, my dears, but this Christmas we're sunk.'

One...

Two...

Three...

KER-PLUNK!

CRACK! went the ice.
'HELP!' Ruby cried...

They dipped and they dived, and they saved every gift.
'At your service,' they bowed. 'Now, would you like a lift?
We can paddle this pond before sunrise, no doubt.
We'll find your friend Santa, and sort this thing out.'

Hey ho!
Here we go!

Go, Flipper and Dipper and Diver and Whisker!
Go, Waddles and Wiggles and Tumbler and Twister!
This round-the-world swim is a stroll in the park!

'Super,' said Ruby.
'But ... is that a—'

Meanwhile, on a beach not too far away...

The first rays of sun crept above the horizon...

And suddenly Rudolf spied something surprising...

A sail?

No! A whale!

'HOT TINSEL! IT'S RUBY!' he yelled with elation.
'My sister! She's guiding a giant cetacean!'

'Hold fast!' Ruby cried.
'Land ahoy!'

'Thar she blows!
Swim for the shore, mates! I see Rudolf's nose!'

Hooray!
To the sleigh!

On, Dasher! On, Dancer! On, Prancer and Vixen!
On, Comet! On, Cupid! On, Donner and Blitzen!
Special delivery! Fly, reindeer, fly!

Bring joy to the world, top to bottom...

Goodbye

First published by Allen & Unwin in 2016

Allen & Unwin – Australia
83 Alexander Street, Crows Nest NSW 2065, Australia
Phone: (61 2) 8425 0100
Email: info@allenandunwin.com
Web: www.allenandunwin.com

Allen & Unwin – UK
Ormond House, 26–27 Boswell Street,
London WC1N 3JZ, UK
Phone: +44 (0) 20 8785 5995
Email: info@murdochbooks.co.uk
Web: www.murdochbooks.co.uk

A Cataloguing-in-Publication entry is available from the
National Library of Australia: www.trove.nla.gov.au.
A catalogue record for this book is available from the British Library.

ISBN (AUS) 978 1 76029 311 6
ISBN (UK) 978 1 74336 921 0

Cover and text design by Nicki Greenberg and Sandra Nobes
Printed in China by Everbest Printing Co., Ltd in July 2016.

1 3 5 7 9 10 8 6 4 2